Curlilocks and the Three Pink Pandas

Told by Yolanda King

Pictures by Fanny Liem

TANGLED
PRESS

For my curly Riley,
handsome Ben and always Babe
- YK

Curlilocks and the Three Pink Pandas
Text Copyright ©2013 by Yolanda King
Illustrations Copyright ©2013 by Tangled Press

Summary: Curlilocks discovers the Pink Pandas' house after getting lost in the Tallest Forest, she explores the Pandas' house without their permission and decides to apologize.

ISBN-0991027213
ISBN-978-0-9910272-1-7

Tangled Press
11824 Jollyville Rd, Ste 302
Austin, TX 78759
www.tangledpress.com

Once there was a little girl with super curly hair named Curlilocks. She lived with her family in a tiny town next to the Tallest Forest.

Saturday was Pancake Day,
and Mom asked Curlilocks to
pick blueberries for breakfast.
"Remember to only pick
berries near the fence,"
warned Mom.

A flutter of butterflies kept her company as she picked the berries. When her new friends began flying away, Curlilocks followed them through the forest.

She and the butterflies danced around a triple twisted oak and hopped on rocks across a tiny stream.

Once they crossed the stream,
Curlilocks looked around.
The fence was nowhere in sight.
She had gone too far.
"Which way is home?"
she wondered.
She felt like
crying.

Nearby, in a pretty yellow cottage, lived a
family of three Pink Pandas. There was Papa Panda,
Momma Panda, and a wee Panda called Pumpkin.

That morning, Momma Panda made a
steaming pot of oatmeal with maple syrup and
ghee. Papa Panda tasted the oatmeal and said,
"Momma, this oatmeal is fantabulous,
but it's too hot. Let's look for ladybugs,
while the oatmeal cools."

Curlilocks noticed the pretty yellow cottage just after the Pandas walked into the woods. She ran to the cottage door and gave three quick knocks. No one answered, but the door swung slowly open. The smell of oatmeal tickled her nose, and Curlilocks quickly forgot Mom's warning not to enter a stranger's house.

She grabbed a spoon
and tasted the big bowl.
"Oh my, this bowl is too swee
She tasted the medium bowl
and said, "Oh no, this is
too salty."

She tasted
the little bowl
and licked her lips.
"This is just right,"
she said and ate every bite.

With a full tummy, Curlilocks began
exploring the cottage. She passed
a large silver mirror and a shelf
with three wooden combs.

She saw that her super curls were super tangled. She tried the biggest comb. "Whoa, these teeth are too loose," she said.

She tried the medium comb and said, "Ouchy, these teeth are too tight."

At last, she tried the little comb and said, "This comb is just right."

She started untangling her curly
locks with such speed and joy that
the small, wooden comb broke in half.

With a happy tummy and
curly hair back in place,
a sleepy Curlilocks continued exploring.
She found the Pandas' three beds.

She quickly hopped off the large bed,
because it was too scratchy.

She slid off the medium bed,
because it was too silky.

She rested on the little Panda's bed and said, "Aha, this bed is just right." Soon she was asleep.

When the three Pink Pandas returned home, they were ravenous. Papa Panda growled, "Someone's been eating my oatmeal."

Momma Panda fussed, " Someone's been eating my oatmeal."

Pumpkin Panda cried, "Someone's been eating my oatmeal, and they've eaten it all up."

Papa Panda looked towards
the mirror and saw the
family combs had been
moved. "Someone's
been using my comb!"
growled Papa Panda.

"Someone's been using my comb!" fussed Momma Panda.

"Someone's been using my comb, and now it's broken!" Pumpkin Panda cried.

The three Pandas were annoyed as they went upstairs.

"Someone's been sleeping in my bed!" growled Papa Panda.

"Someone's been sleeping in my bed!" fussed Momma Panda.

"Someone's been sleeping in my bed," cried Pumpkin Panda, "and she's still snoring on my pillow!"

Just then Curlilocks woke up and
saw the three Pink Pandas.
She let out an "Eek," hopped out of the bed,
and dashed for the open door.

Curlilocks leaped over
the rocks in the stream,
zoomed past the triple
twisted oak, and ran
all the way home.

When she calmed down, she told her parents all about the Panda's house.

Together, they went to apologize to the Pink Panda family.
"I'm really sorry for breaking your comb," Curlilocks said
to Pumpkin Panda. Curlilocks brought Pumpkin
a new comb and helped clean the bedroom.

Then, both families enjoyed a breakfast of blueberry
pancakes, maple syrup, and ghee.

Annoyed - make someone angry

Ghee - clarified butter; it rhymes with key

Panda - member of the bear family, native to China

Ravenous - hungry

Visit us at www.tangledpress.com

f https://www.facebook.com/TangledPress